Ri
and the
Runaway Calf

by Jeff Plum
illustrated by Rosemary Jarman

Harcourt
SCHOOL PUBLISHERS

Printed in China

ISBN 10: 0-15-350535-4
ISBN 13: 978-0-15-350535-5

Ordering Options
ISBN 10: 0-15-350334-3 (Grade 4 Below-Level Collection)
ISBN 13: 978-0-15-350334-4 (Grade 4 Below-Level Collection)
ISBN 10: 0-15-357530-1 (package of 5)
ISBN 13: 978-0-15-357530-3 (package of 5)

5 6 7 8 9 10 985 12 11 10 09

A long time ago in the Wild West lived a cowboy named Pecos Bill. He could do anything other cowboys could do, except he did it a thousand times better. He could ride a tornado as easily as a horse or lasso a hurricane like it was a little calf.

His only equal was Sluefoot Sue. They had so much fun together that they decided to get married. They bought a colossal piece of land that stretched farther than the eye could see. With their son, Rio Rob, they lived as happily as pigs in mud.

One morning, Rio Rob went outside to say hi to Sammy, his favorite calf. Sammy was the fastest calf anyone had ever seen. He could outrun horses, wildcats, and even trains. He could swim mighty rivers and jump over tall tree branches.

This morning, however, Rio Rob made a terrible discovery. Sammy was gone!

Pecos Bill and Sluefoot Sue were just sitting down to a hearty breakfast when Rio Rob burst in the door. He told them the awful news.

"That's mighty bad news, son," said Pecos Bill. "A calf that fast and that strong has probably gotten pretty far."

"There's supposed to be a storm coming," worried Sluefoot Sue. "Sammy might be fast and strong, but that's not going to help him with thunder and lightning out there."

"My pony, Blaze, might be fast enough to catch up to Sammy, Dad," said Rio Rob. "Since Sammy likes me, maybe he'll come if he hears my voice."

Pecos Bill saddled up his horse, Stormy, and Rio Rob jumped on Blaze. They galloped away from the house.

They raced across the many acres that made up Pecos Bill's land. There were rocks, some scattered trees and wildflowers in full bloom. The sky was as blue as a cool ocean. Green waves of grass rippled across the land. It was a scenic view, if you had the time. But Pecos Bill and Rio Rob were too busy searching for Sammy to enjoy it.

Unfortunately, there was no sign of Sammy anywhere. Then Rio Rob heard a strange sound. Thump! Thump! Thump! Rio Rob looked up. A hawk as big as Blaze was diving down from out of the sky. With one swoop, the hawk grabbed Rio Rob's shirt and picked up the pony and the boy!

"Pa! Pa!" Rio Rob hollered.

Blaze kept pawing the air with his hooves as if he was still running on the ground. Rio Rob held on tightly to the reins of the pony.

Pecos Bill and Stormy raced along the ground below. "Hang on!" bellowed Pecos Bill.

When he caught up to the giant bird, Pecos Bill twirled his lasso, threw it up into the air, and looped it around Blaze. As Pecos Bill held tightly to the rope, Rio Rob's shirt ripped, and he and Blaze were free of the hawk. The behemoth bird screamed like a cat with a stepped-on tail and then flew away. Rio Rob and Blaze used Rio Rob's shirt as a parachute, and they floated down like feathers.

Pecos Bill whipped out a needle and thread. He sewed Rio Rob's shirt back together in a lightning-quick second.

"Pa, I saw something while I was up there!" Rio Rob said excitedly. "There's something going on over by the river. Maybe someone's seen Sammy."

They rode over to the river. There weren't any people there, but there were some frogs holding a jumping contest. Some could jump higher than a building. The emerald athletes could jump as far as the Pacific Ocean.

Pecos and Rio approached the frogs. The jumpers greeted them cordially. This might have seemed rather fanciful and odd in another place. However, such chatty animals were common in Pecos Bill's neighborhood. Sure enough, the frogs said they had seen Sammy cross the river a little while ago.

"Be careful," warned a frog. "There's a nasty alligator waiting in the river."

Pecos Bill and Rio Rob set off across the river. The water was so rough that fish jumped up on Blaze and Stormy to get a safe ride across.

At the other side of the river, they shook off the water and tossed back fish. Suddenly, Rio Rob heard a splash, and there was the alligator!

Pecos Bill grabbed the alligator by the tail. Without even using half the energy in his arm, he tossed the alligator all the way to Florida. The alligator landed right in a swamp. It turned out to be a pretty nice place to live, and the alligator was quite happy. Later he sent Pecos Bill a thank-you note.

There was no time to relax, though. Dark clouds were moving closer. Rio Rob thought he saw a tiny dark dot moving in the distance. At first, Rio Rob thought it was an illusion. They had been searching so long that he thought his eyes were playing tricks on him. Then he heard a soft, "Moo!"

"Sammy!" cried Rio Rob.

He and Blaze raced toward the calf with Pecos Bill not far behind. Rio Rob was sure Sammy would be glad to see them. However, when they drew close, the calf ran away!

Rio Rob tried calling Sammy's name and held out some biscuits, but that didn't help. Rio Rob looked at the calf's face as it danced just out of reach. Then Rio Rob had an idea! "Sammy's not trying to run away. He thinks we're playing with him!"

They raced toward Sammy. He ran away again. This time they saw Sammy laughing. Sure enough, he was just having fun!

Rio Rob rode up close to Sammy. Then Rio Rob quickly turned and sped away. Sammy followed, trying to catch up with him.

Pecos Bill snuck up behind the calf with his rope ready. Then he lassoed Sammy and pulled him up on the saddle with him.

"Let's go home, you silly calf!" he shouted.

They raced across the land and made it home in no time. Sluefoot Sue fed a big bale of hay to the hungry calf, and then he fell asleep.

The family went back into the house and settled down. It had been a busy day, but that was common for Pecos Bill, Sluefoot Sue, and Rio Rob.

Think Critically

1. What does "floated down like feathers" mean?
2. Why are Pecos Bill and Rio Rob anxious to catch Sammy?
3. What helped Rio Rob understand what Sammy was doing?
4. How do you think Rio Rob felt when he figured out how to catch Sammy?
5. Would you like to be friends with Rio Rob? Why or why not?

Social Studies

Look It Up This story takes place in the Wild West. Look up information about what parts of the United States made up the Wild West. Then color them in on an outline map of the United States.

School-Home Connection Tell a friend or family member about this story. Then work together to make up your own tall tale.

Word Count: 1,055